For Theresa.

– GLY

For Elena.

– DKK

Duncan's Kingdom

zZZZZz

Zzzzz...
Zz--
Eh?
CROAK!
WAK
HUFF PUFF

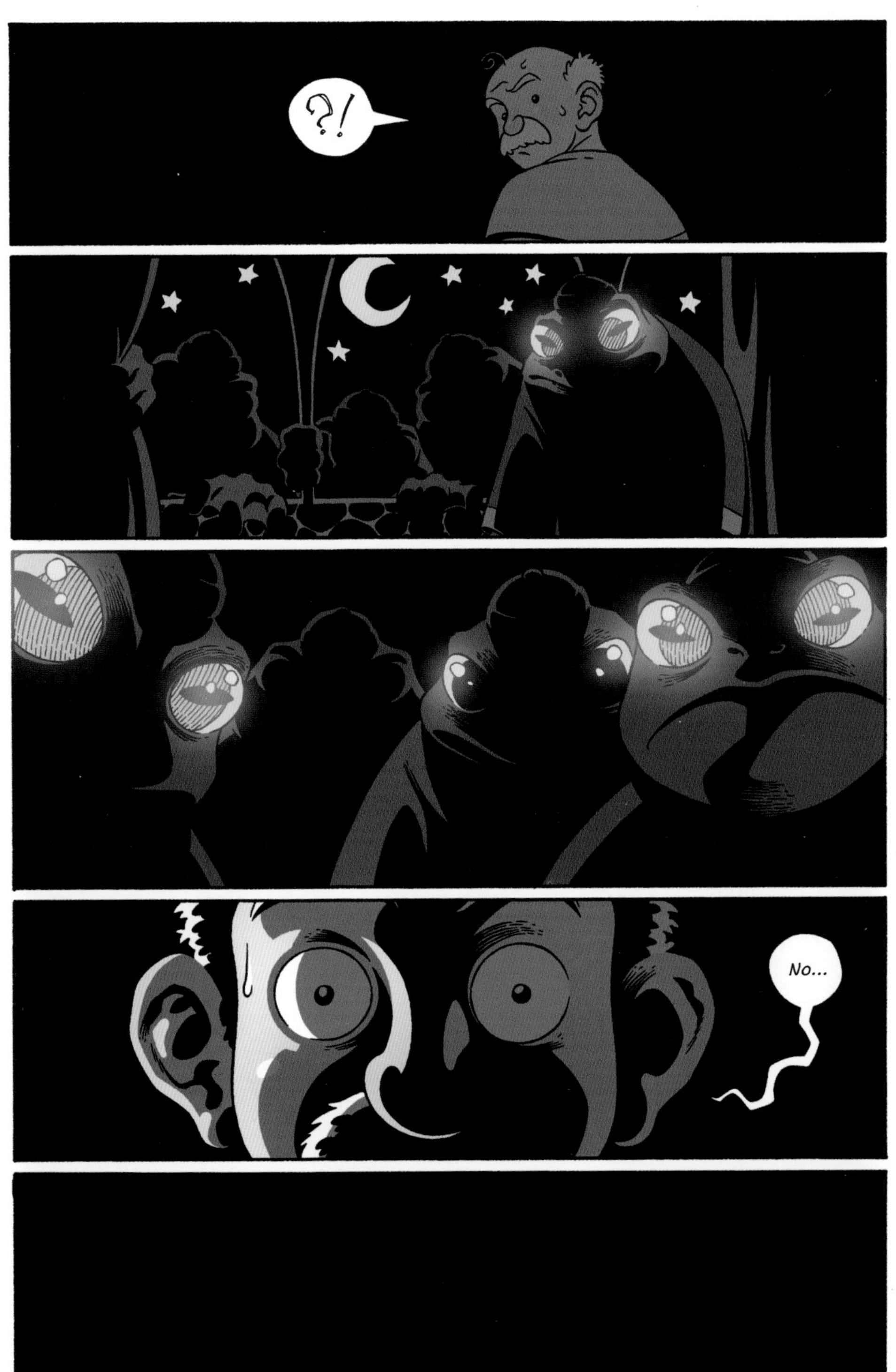
?!
No...

Your eyes glisten like wet marbles...
Tee hee!

Your cheeks are soft, like the bellies of newborn rabbits...
Ha ha!

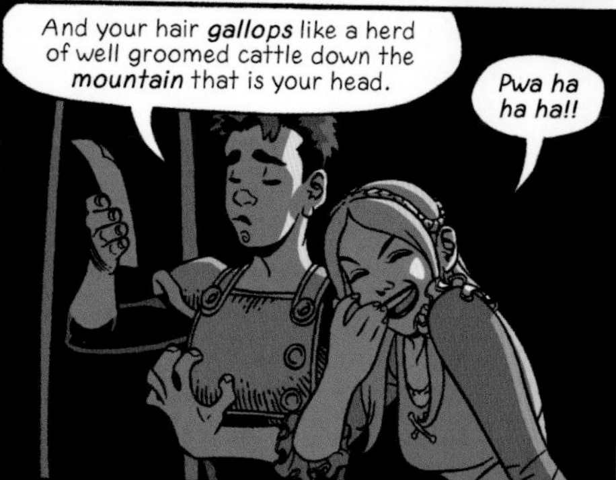
And your hair gallops like a herd of well groomed cattle down the mountain that is your head.
Pwa ha ha ha!!

Oh!
Will you just kiss me please?
Why didn't you just ask in the first place?

Your Highness?

Your Highness... It's the King...

Men of the Royal Guard... The *Frog King* has devastated my family and humiliated our kingdom.
My father's death must be ***avenged.***

I want the Frog King's head.
Whoever among you can do this for me shall be my ***husband...***
...and our *new king.*

AAAH!

Duncan! What's wrong?
Brother Patchwork!

It's... It's nothing. It's just that silly dream again.

With the *lady?*
Yes...

I just always get the feeling... that I *owe* her something.

Do you have any idea what?
I... I don't know.

I'm going to the *Swamp Lands* tomorrow.
I know. To retrieve the *head* of the *Frog King*.
... The princess doubts me...
Yes. I know that too.

Are you *scared*, Duncan?
Of the *Frog King*? No. But the *swamp*...
That's where I *found* you so many years ago.

And that's why it *scares* me. I can't remember a *thing* before the day I met you.

I have something for you, Duncan.

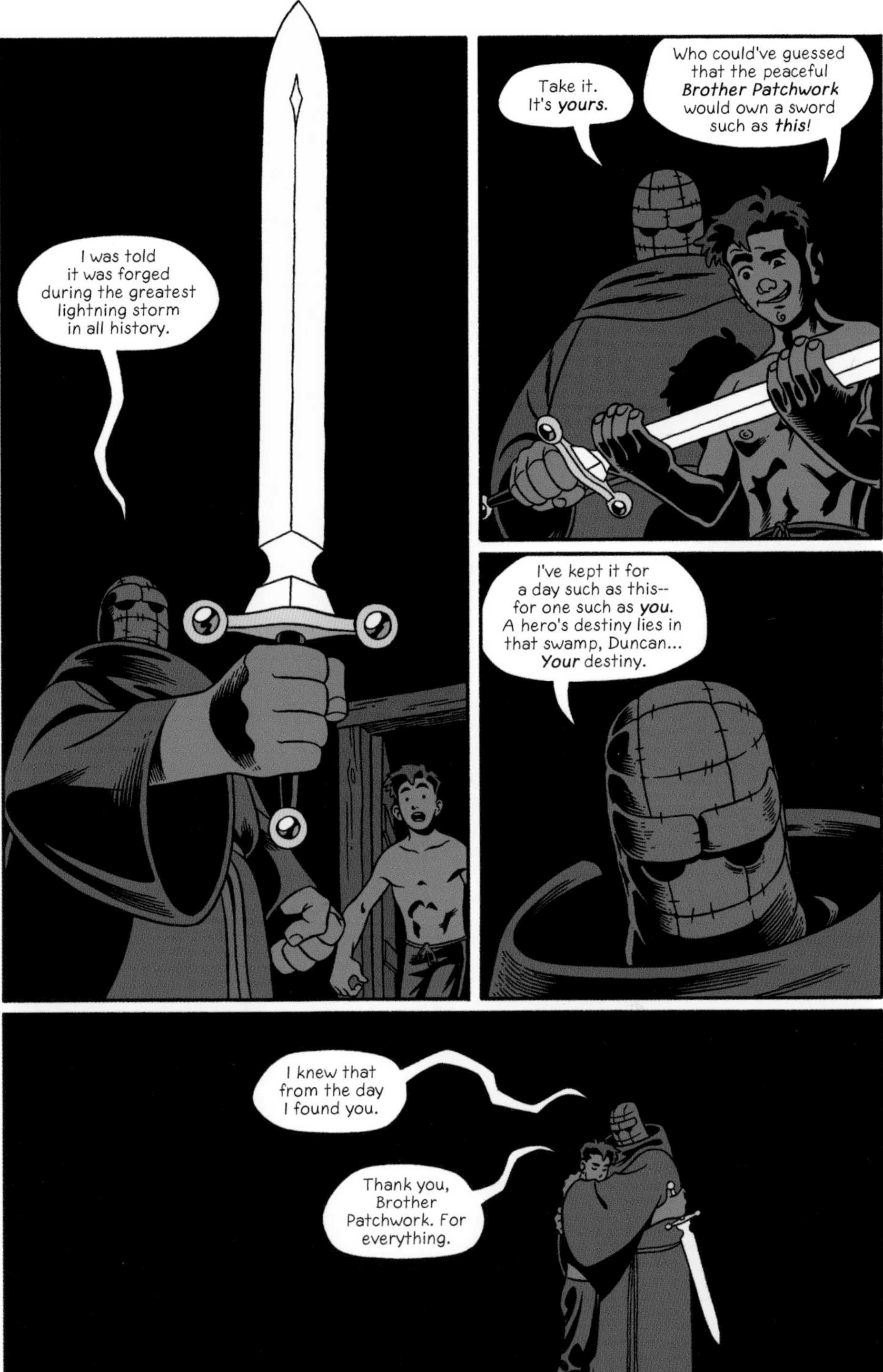
I was told it was forged during the greatest lightning storm in all history.
Take it. It's *yours.*
Who could've guessed that the peaceful *Brother Patchwork* would own a sword such as *this!*
I've kept it for a day such as this-- for one such as *you.* A hero's destiny lies in that swamp, Duncan... *Your* destiny.
I knew that from the day I found you.
Thank you, Brother Patchwork. For everything.

Ack!

Koff!
Cough!
Ptoo!

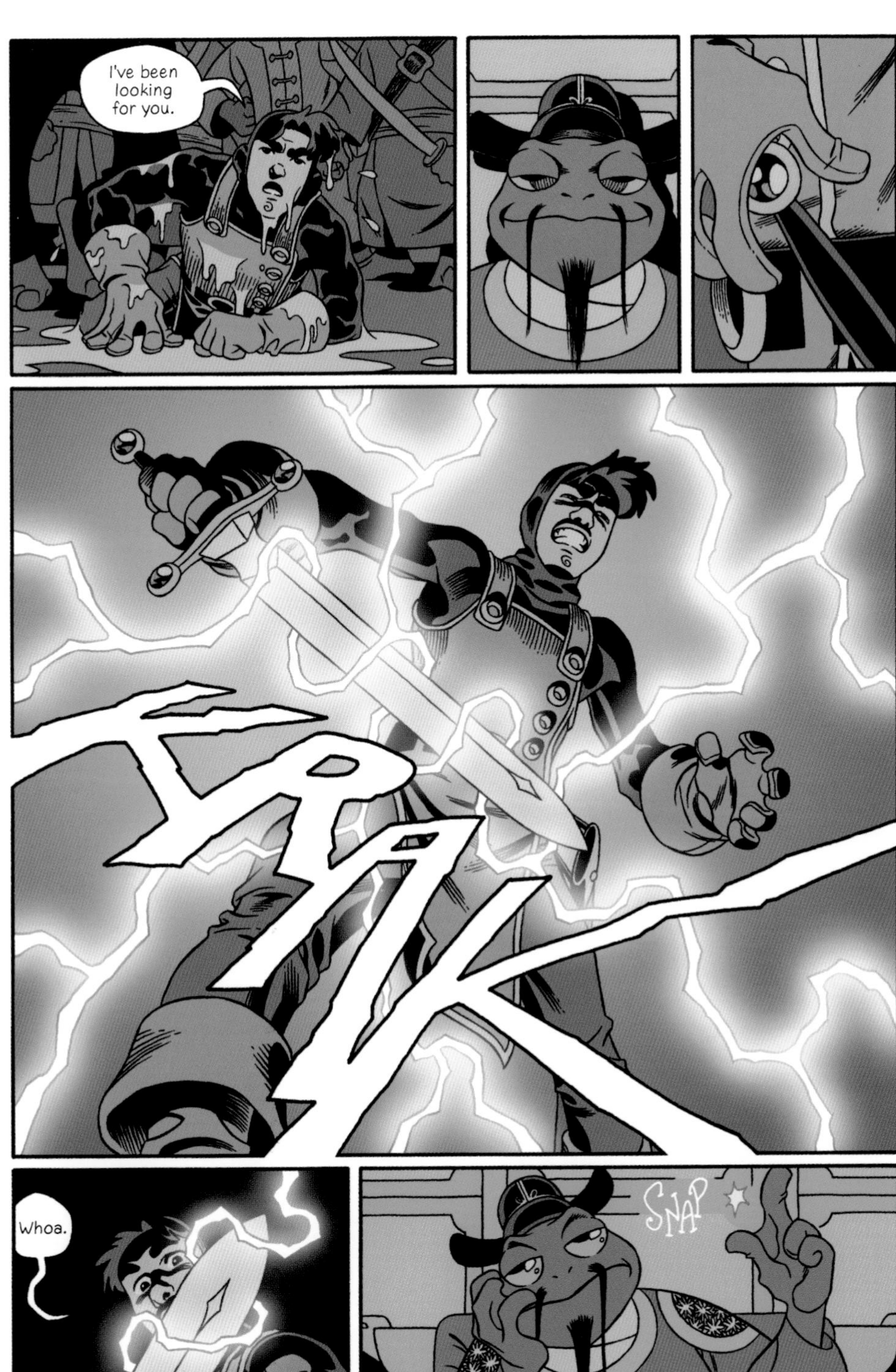
I've been looking for you.
KRAK
Whoa.
SNAP

krackle
This is for the King!
crackle
krak
Whoa!

Thanks, boy! I can take it from here!

Gnnh!

SLAM!

CRACK
KRAK

CRUMBLE
TOK
Ow!

Ha! So much for the great Frog Ki--

EEEYAH!

Listen, boy!

You musn't--
You--
You *talk*?!

Please--
I offer you my *head*, as long as you promise to *leave immediately.*
Do you promise?

Uh...
Sure.

Now remember, boy...

A *hero* never breaks his promises.
SLICE

BOUNCE
BOUNCE

CRACK
CRACK
KRAK
KRAK!

Snappy
Cola

CLAP!
CHEER
WOOHOO
YEAH!

CHEER
YAY

Duncan...

I'm sorry.
I'm sorry I ever doubted you.

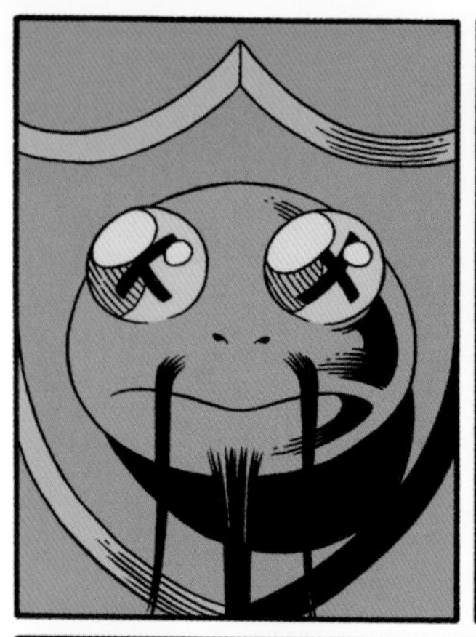

AUTOGRAPH BOOK

Come here.
I still owe you that kiss.

Snappy Cola
You should be in bed, Duncan.
Good evening, Brother Patchwork.
Where did you find this?!
What? The Frog King had it--
GRAB
What're you doing?!
Snappy Cola

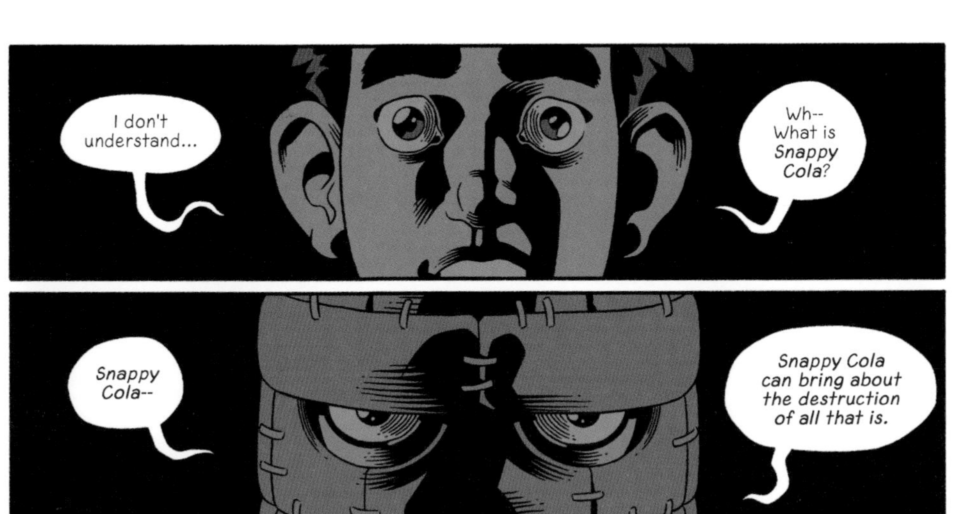

I don't understand...
Wh-- What is *Snappy Cola*?

Snappy Cola--

Snappy Cola can bring about the destruction of all that is.

I'm sorry, Duncan...
It's just that I've seen things-- ***experienced*** things-- that I would never wish upon anyone, especially ***you***.

Besides, you really should be in bed.
You'll be receiving both a wife and a crown tomorrow.
B-but Brother--

Come now, Duncan. A ***hero*** needs his rest.

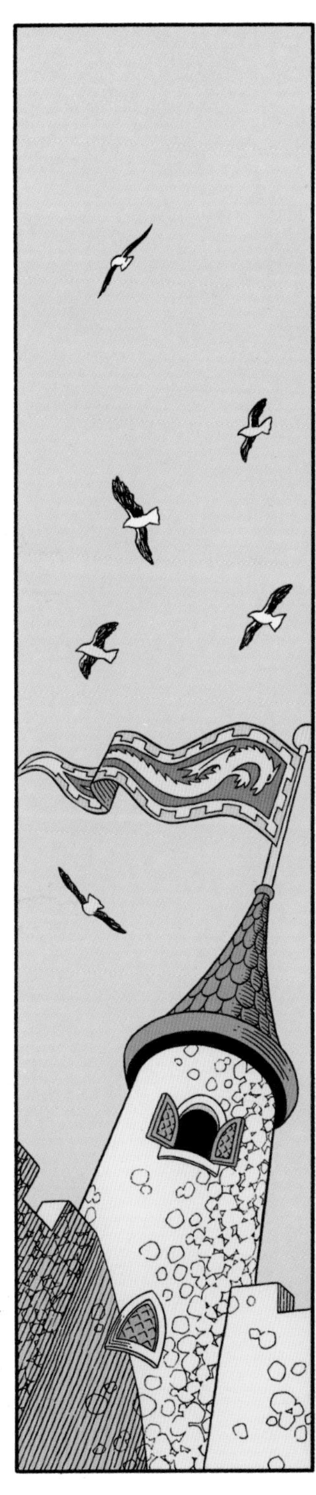

Dearly beloved, our gathering here today is truly one of utmost privilege...

...for we bear witness not only to the union of two blessed souls...
SQUAK

...but also to the birth of a new era for this glorious kingdom...

Well, sire? *Do* you or do you *not*?

Forgive me, sire, but perhaps it would behoove you to *pay attention.*
This is, after all, ***your wedding.***

Duncan!

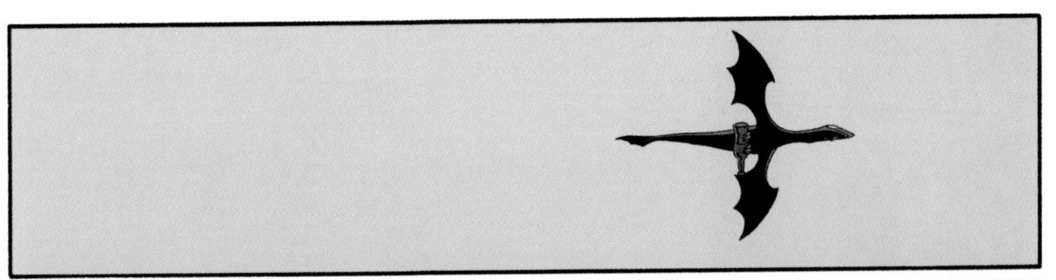

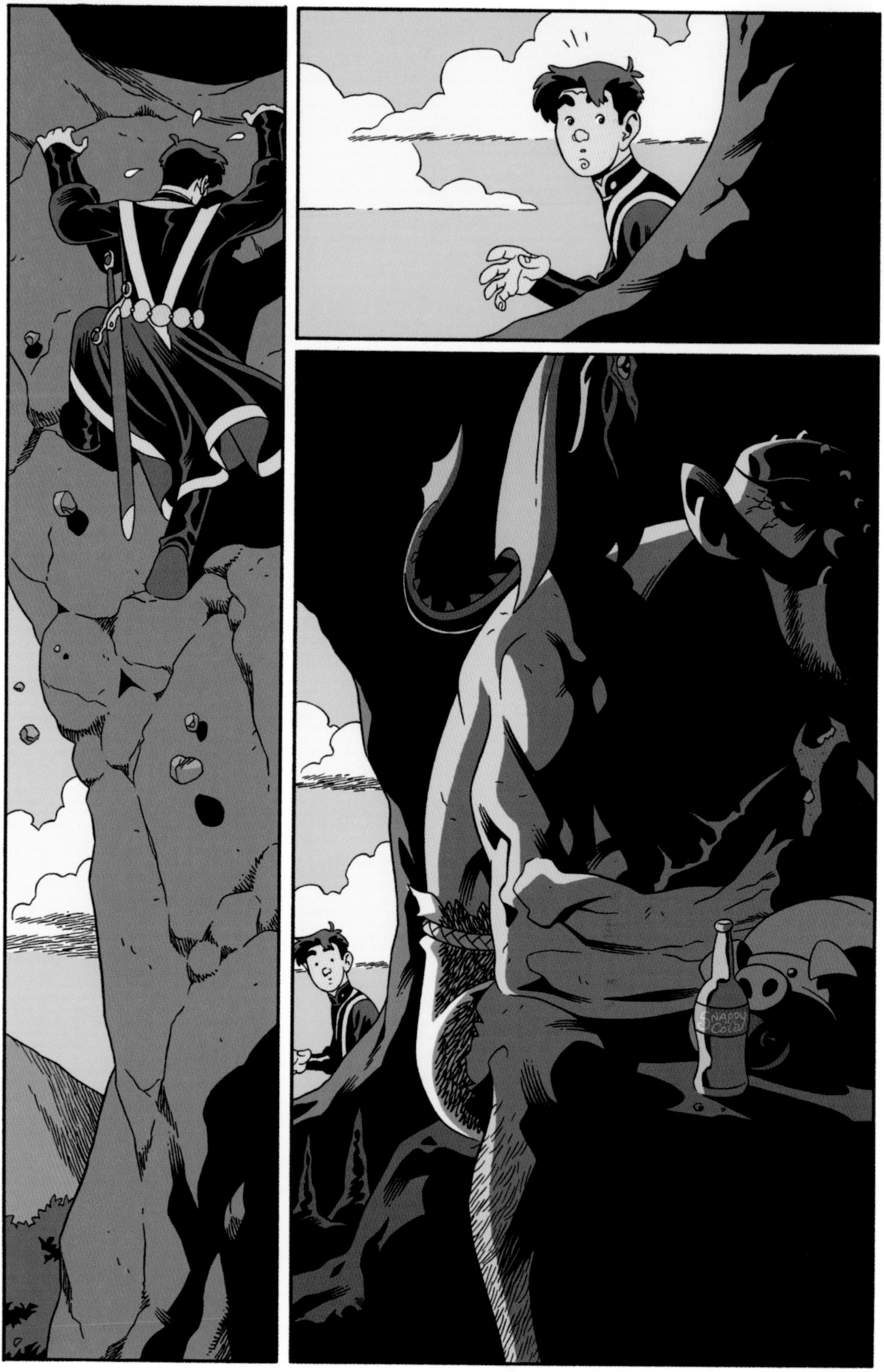

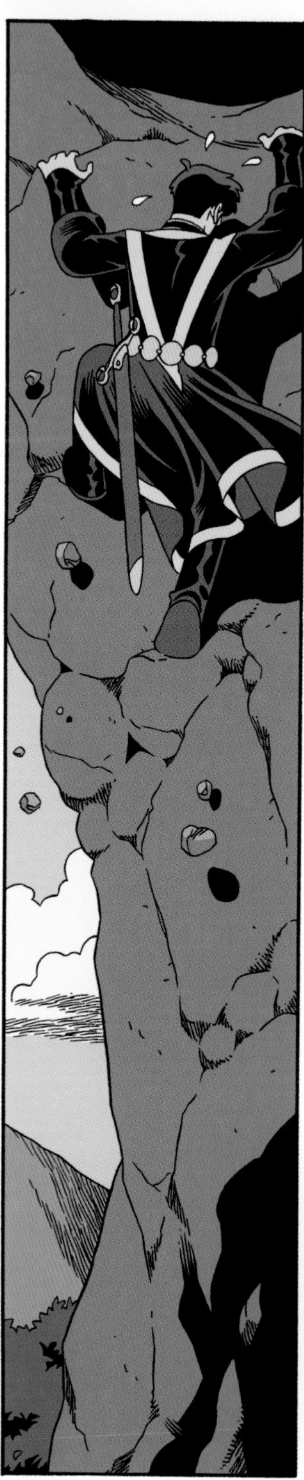

YOU DISTURB ME.
...
I want that bottle.
SNAPPY COLA BELONGS TO ME.
NOW LEAVE.
I want that bottle!

YOU DARE TRY MY PATIENCE, PUNY INSECT?! I'LL CRUSH YOUR SKULL AND FEAST ON YOUR FLESH!
I'LL PICK MY TEETH WITH YOUR SCRAWNY BONES!

We'll see about that, big boy!
KRAK

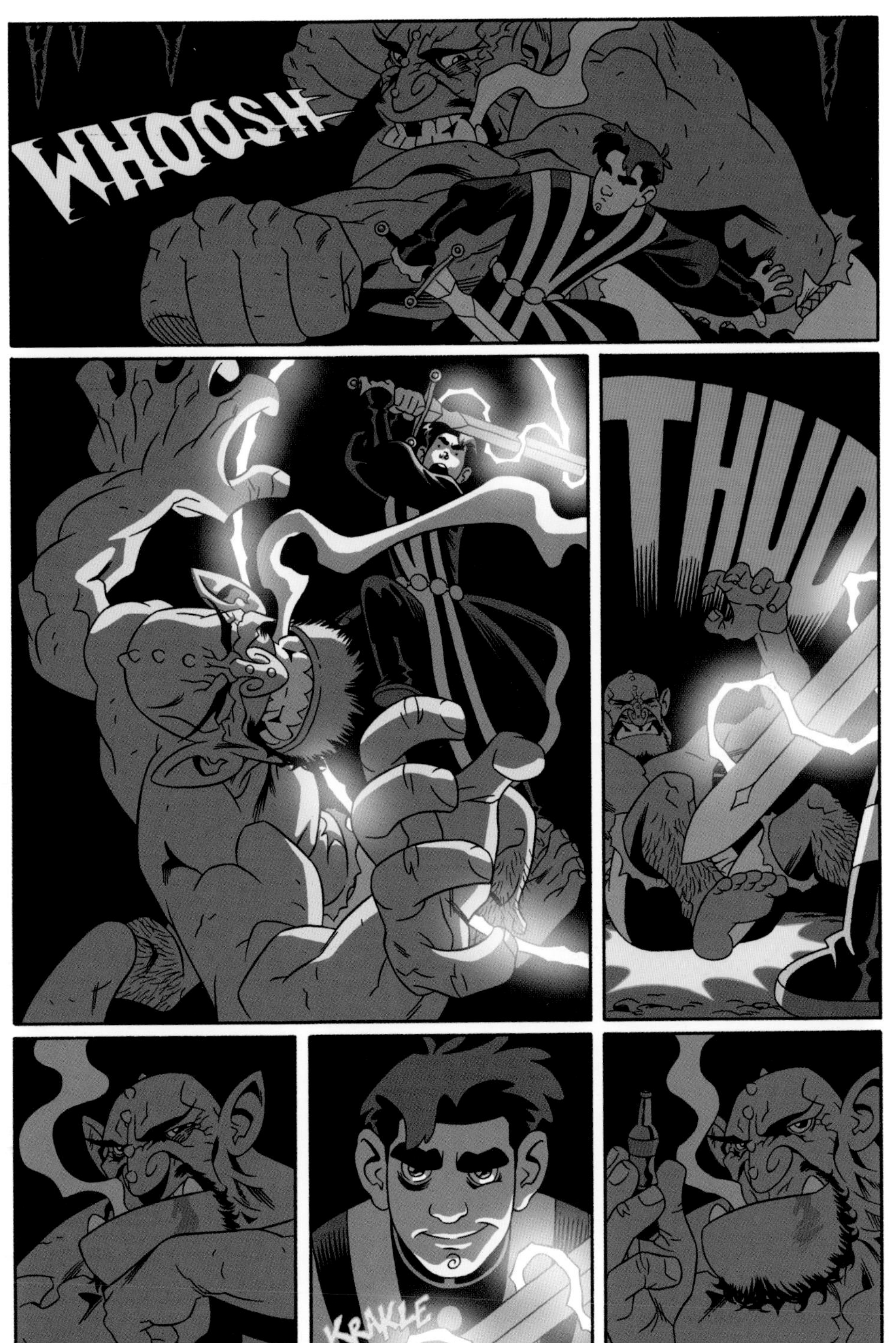
WHOOSH
THUD
KRAKLE

KRAK

No!

SPLORCH
Why can't you just leave it alone?
Who said that?
You have a wife and a kingdom waiting for you, for crying out loud!
What else do you need? What more could you possibly want?!
Take the giant's head and go home.
You'll be a greater hero than you ever were -- than you've ever dreamed.
Who are you?

...
B-Brother Patchwork?

I'm giving you the chance to be a *hero*, Duncan.
And you're *blowing* it.

I- I don't understand...

I *created* those enemies for you! And I gave you the weapon you needed to *destroy* them! All you had to do was bring home a head or two, and you can't even get *that* right!
You *created* the Frog King?
Yes!

Then you-- You're *responsible* for the King's death?!

Responsible for the king's death?!
Duncan, I made the King!

Who are you?!

No! What do you think you're--?!

What's going on?!
KRAK

Put that away.
WAP

This is how you show your *gratitude* to the person who's giving you everything you've ever wanted?

What I want is the truth.

The "truth."
All right.

The "truth" is, Duncan, you don't live in a magical kingdom, you live in a tenement in Oakland. And your world isn't filled with kings and castles and princesses -- it's filled with politicians, concrete buildings, and girls who won't give you the time of day.

OAK PARK APARTMENTS

And in all "truthfulness," Duncan, you're not a knight in the royal guard. You're a loser. You have no friends. You spend most of your waking hours with your nose buried in your books, your comics, and your porno mags.

You're lying!

I am, am I?
Then how is it that you know what a porno mag is?

Have I mentioned that *girl* you've had a crush on since the *third grade*? She must've inspired an encyclopedia's worth of *poetry* from you -- all *drivel* -- and yet you haven't spoken a single word to her.
Imagine that.

Not that it'd *matter.* Rumor has it she recently started dating one of those *varsity water polo types* -- big, tall, strapping boy with a nice sports car.
The very picture of *virility.*

All this and we haven't even gotten to the *juicy parts.*
Isn't the "truth" just *dandy*?

Your birth father was a zoologist. He died two years ago from salmonella. Seems he forgot to wash his hands after experimenting with a batch of rare Asian frogs. ≡tsk tsk≡
Since then you've had a veritable police line-up of would-be "father figures." The latest is a chain-smoking bartender. Every time your mother messes up the pancakes, he beats her 'til she squeals like a pig.
When you tried to stop him last week, he beat you into a coma.
That's how we met.
And your mother -- isn't she something! She hasn't held down a steady job for the past two years because of her "headaches."
Besides, most of her time is taken up by her duties as the president of the Snappy Cola Fan Club.

Your mother is a *pathetic little creature* living a *pathetic little life.*
I can't kick him out, Duncan. He pays all the *bills.*
Well, if you're not going to do it, I'll do it for you.
You said so yourself just before I *found* you.
You know, Ma, sometimes I think you *deserve* to get *smacked around.*
Is that what you *wanted*, Duncan?
Is that enough *"truth"* for you?

Do you understand now? I'm not trying to *hide* the truth from you--
--I'm just... *rearranging* it so that it doesn't *hurt* and *embarrass* you so much.

...

Look. Maybe this whole fantasy angle is a bit *hokey.* Maybe we should try something *new.*

How about being the captain of your own *starship?*

Or what if we gave you a *cape*, some *super-powers*, and a *metropolis* to defend?

Or perhaps the *playboy* lifestyle is more suited to your *needs*.

What I'm *trying* to say is that I can *give* you whatever you *want*.
Just *name* it. It's my *job*.

...

NAPPA
Cola

Well? What do you say?

I... I have to *go back*.
I owe my mom an *apology*.

But don't you get it by now? That's the beauty of being with me! You never have to apologize!
You win all the battles! Vanquish all your enemies! Get all the girls! You're a hero, Duncan! What is there to apologize for?

...

You make me sick, you know that?
I offer you the chance to be a hero, and instead you want to be a mama's boy.

W- wait-- Hold on, Duncan! Where're you going?!

You're not leaving me!

Please, Duncan! I need y--
We-- We need each other.

Get away from me.

You don't know what you're *saying*, Duncan. ***You're beside yourself.***

I'm the ***only one*** who truly ***cares*** for you, don't you see that?! The only one who truly ***loves***--

SLICE
Get away from me!

SLIC
Get away from me!

SNAPPY Cola

KRAK

Ma?

Oh God.

I've been so *worried* for the past few days! I've been so... so *lonely*...

Ma-- I'm *sorry*.
What?
About what I said *before* all this, about you *deserving*--

Shush, Honey.
Just shush.

HOSPITAL

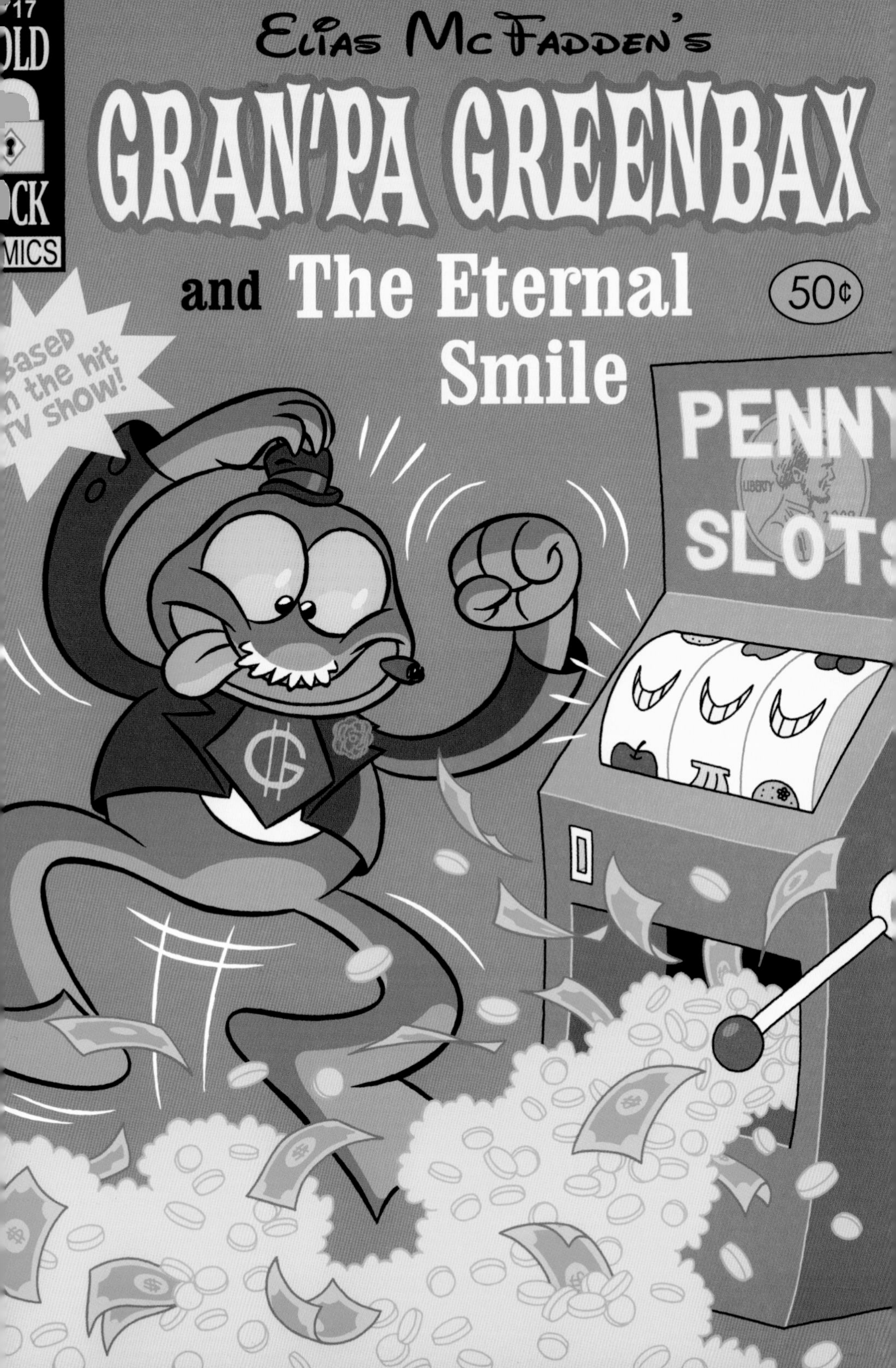

17
OLD
OCK
MICS
Elias McFadden's
GRAN'PA GREENBAX
and The Eternal Smile
50¢
Based on the hit TV show!
PENNY SLOTS
LIBERTY

FROGVILLE, USA! GRAN'PA GREENBAX WATCHES EAGERLY AS THE SPOILS OF HIS LATEST PROFITABLE ADVENTURE POUR INTO HIS LEGENDARY ***POOL O' CASH!***

CAREFUL NOT TO LOSE A SINGLE PENNY, ***FILBERT!***

I-I-I'M D-DOING MY B-BEST, SIR!

GRAN'PA GREENBAX and THE ETERNAL SMILE

AH! NOTHING TICKLES YOUR EARS LIKE THE SOUND OF COINAGE IN THE MORNING, EH, GIRLS?
YOU BETCHA, GRAN'PA GREENBAX!

GRAN'PA SURE MADE A ***LOTTA*** MONEY SELLIN' SHOE POLISH TO THE PINEAPPLE ISLAND PYGMIES, ***POLLY!***
HE SURE DID, 'SPECIALLY CONSIDERIN' THE PYGMIES DON'T EVEN WEAR SHOES! D'YA THINK HE FINALLY HAS ENOUGH?

WE'RE ABOUT TO FIND OUT!
LOOK OUT BELOW!

GO, GRAN'PA, ***GO!***
SPLASH

CROOOOOOOOOOOAK!

?
KEEP OUT!
THAT MEANS YOU!
YES, YOU!

THIS SECOND-RATE SWIMMING HOLE HAS BUSTED MY POOR NOSE ***ONCE AGAIN!*** ALL I WANT IS FOR IT TO BE DEEP ENOUGH SO I WON'T HIT BOTTOM WHEN I DIVE! IS THAT SO MUCH TO ASK?!

FILBERT! FIND ME ANOTHER PROFITABLE ADVENTURE, ***ON THE DOUBLE!***
I-I'M ON IT, S-SIR!

W-WELL, MY RESEARCH INDICATES TH-THERE MIGHT BE RICH V-VEINS OF G-GOLD BENEATH THE I-ICELANDIA ICE CAPS!

I BOUGHT ICELANDIA AND EXCAVATED EVERY LAST NUGGET OF GOLD LAST MONDAY! ***NEXT!***

L-LOCAL LEGENDS IN C-CALIJUANA TELL OF A MAGICAL TR-TREE THAT BEARS ***P-P-PIGS*** INSTEAD OF F-FRUIT!

WE FOUND THAT TREE LAST TUESDAY AND MY BACON FACTORY'S ALREADY SAVED A FORTUNE! ***NEXT!***

W-WORD ON THE STREET IS THAT A NEW STYLE OF M-M-MUSIC IS CAUSING Q-QUITE THE ST-STIR AMONG YOUNGSTERS--

NOTORIOUS P.I.G.! SNOOP FROGGY FROG! EMINEMU! SIGNED AND EXPLOITED THEM ALL LAST WEDNESDAY, THURSDAY, AND FRIDAY!

FILBERT, YOU LOUT! IF YOU DON'T FIND ME SOMETHING FAST, I'LL CUT YOUR SALARY ***IN HALF!***

B-BUT I ONLY MAKE ***3 CENTS*** AN H-H-HOUR!

AND I'LL ROUND DOWN, TOO!

WELL, TH-TH-THERE IS ONE M-MORE ITEM ON MY L-LIST...
SIX HOURS LATER, THE FROGS FIND THEMSELVES IN THE MIDDLE OF THE DESERT JUST NORTH OF FROGVILLE!
THIS HAD BETTER BE GOOD, FILBERT! I'VE ALREADY USED $32.06 IN GAS AND 73 CENTS IN SHOE SOLE!
YEAH, FILBERT!

I-I J-J-JUST WANTED TO SH-SHOW YOU TH-TH-THAT.

OOOOH.
WHAT *IS* IT?

I-I FOUND IT A FEW M-MONTHS B-B-BACK, WHEN I WAS L-LOOKING FOR S-SOMEPLACE TO BE ALONE. I-I'VE BEEN ST-STUDYING IT SINCE, AND I STILL D-D-DON'T KNOW WHAT IT IS.

IT'S NOT AN O-O-OPTICAL ILLUSION O-OR A C-C-CLOUD FORMATION OR A M-MAN-MADE STRUCTURE. TH-TH-THERE'S REALLY N-N-NO SCIENTIFIC EXPLANATION FOR ITS EX-EXISTENCE.
AAAAH.

HOW'S IT GOING TO MAKE ME *MONEY?!*
YEAH, HOW'S IT GONNA MAKE GRAN'PA MONEY?!

SOMETIMES, D-D-DEEP DOWN INSIDE, I GET TH-THIS... THIS *L-LONGING* FOR LIFE... OR MAYBE THE W-WORLD... OR MAYBE MY OWN B-B-BEING TO BE MORE THAN IT ACTUALLY IS.
I'M N-NOT SURE WHY, BUT WH-WH-WHEN I L-LOOK AT THAT... THAT ETERNAL SMILE... MY LONGING GETS S-SATISFIED FOR A B-B-BIT. I FEEL AT P-P-PEACE.

I WAS H-H-HOPING YOU'D FEEL P-PEACE HERE, TOO, SO YOU WOULDN'T C-CUT MY S-S-SALARY.
ETERNAL SMILE?!

TH-THAT'S SORT OF WHAT I N-N-NAMED IT.
CROAK!

YOU TWIT! THE TEN CENTS OF SHOE SOLE IT'LL TAKE TO KICK YOUR PATOOTIE WILL BE MY MOST WORTHWHILE EXPENSE TODAY!

ACK!

COUGH! COUGH!
YOU DRAGGED ME ALL THE WAY OUT HERE FOR THIS?! I WANT MONEY, FILBERT, NOT YOUR GOOFY RELIGIOUS MUMBO-JUMBO! WHO IN TARNATION HAS EVER HEARD OF RELIGION MAKING ANYBODY--

--MONEY?
$KA-CHING$

THAT'S IT, FILBERT! THIS WILL BE MY MOST PROFITABLE ADVENTURE YET! WE'LL BUILD A CHURCH AND PEOPLE WILL FLOCK TO US WITH THEIR POCKETBOOKS!

WE'LL BUILD THE CHURCH OF THE ETERNAL SMILE!
YAY!

SO D-DOES TH-TH-THIS MEAN I GET TO K-K-KEEP MY SALARY?

OVER THE NEXT WEEK, GRAN'PA GREENBAX OVERSEES THE CONSTRUCTION OF HIS NEW CHURCH!
MAKE IT GRAND, FELLAS! GRAND ENOUGH TO INSPIRE GENEROUS DONATIONS!

HOW'RE THINGS GOING HERE, GIRLS?
WE'RE JUST 'BOUT FINISHED SEWIN' THE PRIESTLY GARMENTS, GRAN'PA!

WONDERFUL, BECAUSE IT'S HIGH TIME WE START EVANGELIZING!
$
$

SOON, MOLLY AND POLLY ARE SPREADING GRAN'PA GREENBAX'S GOOD NEWS ON THE STREETS OF FROGVILLE!
LONELY? TIRED? HAD A BAD DAY?
LET THE ETERNAL SMILE SHOW YOU THE WAY!

SAY, AREN'T YOU MR. GREENBAX'S LITTLE GRANDDAUGHTERS?
WHY, YES WE ARE, SIR! AND WE'RE STARTIN' A BRAND-NEW CHURCH!

A CHURCH FOUNDED BY LITTLE GIRLS?
UH... WELL...
IT'S NOT REALLY FOUNDED BY US, SIR, BUT BY THE DIVINE WILL OF THE ETERNAL SMILE!

HMMM...
GOOD THINKIN', POLLY!
THANKS, MOLLY!

DON'T LOOK NOW, BUT HERE COMES TROUBLE!
NO SOLICITING! NO SOLICITING!

CAN'T YOU LITTLE HOOLIGANS READ? NO SOLICITING!
NO SOLICITING

NO SOLICITING

HOLY TOLEDO, YOU'RE FAT, MA'AM!
SOB! IT'S TRUE!

AND MY HOSTILITY TOWARD YOU GIRLS IS ONLY A COVER FOR MY OWN LACK OF SELF-ESTEEM!
THERE, THERE. COME LET THE ETERNAL SMILE TAKE ALL YOUR PAIN AWAY.
honk!

AT LONG LAST, THE CHURCH OF THE ETERNAL SMILE OPENS ITS DOORS TO THE PUBLIC!

LOOK AT ALL THESE PEOPLE! YOU GIRLS DESERVE A RAISE!
YA MEAN IT?
NO.

MAY THE ETERNAL SMILE SHINE DOWN UPON US ALL.
WELCOME, MY BROTHERS AND SISTERS! PEACE OF THE ETERNAL SMILE BE WITH YOU!

NOW BROTHER FILBERT, IF YOU WOULD KINDLY PASS THE COLLECTION BASKET--
WHAT?! WHAT KIND OF COCKAMAMIE CHURCH IS THIS?!

YOU CAN'T START COLLECTIN' STRAIGHT AWAY, GRAN'PA GREENBAX! YOU'VE GOTTA GIVE THE PEOPLE A SERMON OR A READING FIRST!
A READING?! WHERE AM I GONNA GET--

WAIT A MINUTE! WHAT ABOUT THAT LITTLE BOOK YOU GIRLS ARE ALWAYS CARRYING AROUND?
THE LI'L MUFFINS SCOUTING GUIDE?! WE CAN'T SHOW THAT TO YOU!
WE TOOK A VOW!

I'LL GIVE YOU THAT RAISE!
DEAL!

AHEM. TO START A CAMPFIRE, ARRANGE SEVERAL TWIGS IN A TEEPEE FORMATION. THEN PLACE--
WHAT IS THIS PATOOEY?!

THAT "PATOOEY" IS ONLY THE BEST CAMPFIRE ADVICE ON THE PLANET!
YOU OUGHTA SHOW SOME RESPECT, MISTER!
WHY DON'T YOU COME MAKE ME?!

GIRLS, PLEASE! YOU'RE BEATING UP MY CUSTOMERS-- I MEAN, CONGREGATION!
BAM!
BIFF!
POW!

ST-ST-STOP!

TH-THIS ISN'T HOW IT'S S-S-SUPPOSED TO BE!

CAN'T YOU P-P-PEOPLE SEE THE ET-ETERNAL SMILE'S S-S-SIGNIFICANCE?! THERE'S NO EXPLANATION F-F-FOR IT! EXCEPT P-PERHAPS...
...
YOU KNOW, I USED TO COME HERE WH-WH-WHENEVER I FELT OP-OPPRESSED BY MY--
...UH, L-LIFE.
!

SEEING THE ETERNAL SM-SMILE W-W-WOULD G-GIVE ME HOPE-- HOPE THAT MAYBE, J-J-JUST MAYBE, THE UNDER-LYING PR-PRINCIPLE OF THE UNIVERSE ISN'T M-M-MONOTONY OR FEAR OR C-COMPETITION, BUT J-JOY.

I'D W-WONDER IF THE ETERNAL SM-SM-SMILE WAS THE SM-SMILE OF EXISTENCE IT-ITSELF. AND IF EXISTENCE ITSELF C-COULD SM-SM-SMILE, THEN M-MAYBE S-S-SOMEDAY I WOULD TOO.

THAT GOOD-FOR-NOTHING INGRATE! I OUGHTA--
WAIT, GRAN'PA!
LOOK!

THE CONGREGATION RESPONDS GENEROUSLY TO FILBERT'S TESTIMONY!
BOO HOO!
WHERE'S THAT COLLECTION BASKET?

HA HA!
BUT WAIT! WHO'S THAT MYSTERIOUS FIGURE GOING OUT THE BACK DOOR?!

THAT NIGHT, GRAN'PA GREENBAX AND FILBERT TALLY UP THE DAY'S HAUL!
F-F-FOUR HUNDRED KA-KAJILLION AND ONE, FOUR H-HUNDRED KAJILLION AND TWO...
HA HA! YOUR RANT MUST'VE DONE A NUMBER ON THEIR HEARTSTRINGS, FILBERT!

A FULL WEEK OF SERVICES LIKE THIS AND MY ***POOL O' CASH*** WILL BE DEEP ENOUGH FOR SURE!
SEMPITERNUS RISUS UTINAM LAUDARERIS...

THE CROWD IS ***GONE***, GIRLS. YOU CAN STOP NOW.
NO WE ***CAN'T***, GRAN'PA.
THE ETERNAL SMILE DESERVES-- NO, ***DEMANDS***-- OUR PERPETUAL ADORATION.

SEMPITERNUS RISUS UTINAM LAUDARERIS...
scritch scritch
?

... YOU KNOW, FILBERT, I HAVE A CONFESSION TO MAKE. WHEN WE WERE OUT IN THE DESERT, YOU TALKED ABOUT A LONGING FOR MORE FROM LIFE.
I DIDN'T WANT TO ADMIT IT... BUT I'VE FELT THAT LONGING BEFORE. I'VE LOOKED FOR WAYS TO SATISFY IT, TOO.

I'VE LOOKED HIGH AND LOW, ALL AROUND THE WORLD. WHY DO YOU THINK I EVEN STARTED GOING ON PROFITABLE ADVENTURES?
AND IN ALL MY TRAVELS, I'VE FOUND ONLY ***ONE THING*** THAT EVEN COMES CLOSE TO SATISFYING THAT LONGING.
WHAT'S THAT, SIR?

MONEY. A BIG, GOLDEN POOL OF IT, DEEP ENOUGH TO DIVE INTO AND NEVER HIT BOTTOM! THAT'S THE ANSWER TO YOUR LONGING, BOY, NOT SOME SILLY SHAPE IN THE SKY!

B-BUT, SIR--
NOW HELP ME COUNT THE REST OF THIS! AND KEEP YOUR HANDS WHERE I CAN SEE THEM!

EARLY THE NEXT MORNING, GRAN'PA GREENBAX IS GREETED WITH AN UNEXPECTED -- AND *UNPROFITABLE* -- SURPRISE!
THE SERVICE IS ABOUT TO START IN *TEN MINUTES!* WHERE'S MY CONGREGATION?!
I'M N-NOT SURE, SIR!

LOOK, GRAN'PA!

MEMBERS OF GRAN'PA GREENBAX'S CONGREGATION FLOCK TO A MASSIVE *TENT* JUST OUTSIDE HIS CHURCH!
CROAK!
YOU GOTTA HEAR THIS FELLOW!

INSIDE THE TENT IS NONE OTHER THAN GRAN'PA GREENBAX'S ARCHRIVAL--
SKINFLINT O'GERBIL! I SHOULD'VE KNOWN!

OUR SMILE IS A *GENEROUS* SMILE, AND ALL OF CREATION IS SUBJECT TO ITS GLORIOUS COUNTENANCE!
THE SMILE WANTS YOU TO BE *HAPPY*, BROTHERS AND SISTERS! AND IT WANTS YOU TO BE *RICH!* GIVE THE SMILE YOUR FAITH AND IT WILL GIVE YOU YOUR HEARTS' DEEPEST *DESIRES!*

AND THAT'S WHY I'M OFFERING THESE GOLD-PLATED ETERNAL SMILE *LAPEL PINS!* WEAR THEM AS A *VISIBLE TESTAMENT* TO YOUR FAITH! ONLY $29.95 APIECE!
OUT OF MY WAY!

CROAK! HOW CAN YOU PEOPLE STAND TO LISTEN TO THIS TWO-BIT *COPYCAT?!*

AH, GREENBAX! HAVE YOU FINALLY COME TO CONFESS THE TRUTH?
WHAT ARE YOU YAMMERING ABOUT, YOU WEASEL?!

WHAT?! SO YOU'RE DENYING THAT YOUR WEALTH IS A DIRECT RESULT OF YOUR FAITH IN THE ETERNAL SMILE?!
WHA-?!

A FAITH THAT CAN BE AMPLY EXPRESSED BY THIS GOLD-PLATED ETERNAL SMILE LAPEL PIN, AVAILABLE FOR ONLY $29.95!
POPPYCOCK! YOU KNOW AS WELL AS ANYBODY THAT NOTHING BUT OLD-FASHIONED ELBOW GREASE AND SHAMELESS EXPLOITATION CAN MAKE YOU MONEY, O'GERBIL!

YOU PEOPLE DON'T ACTUALLY BELIEVE THIS OLD COOT, DO YOU?!

BOOT!

OH, WHAT AM I GOING TO DO?! THAT SCOUNDREL'S LURED AWAY MY FLOCK, AND HIS DASTARDLY LAPEL PINS ARE SELLING LIKE HOTCAKES!

AND BY HOLDING SERVICES IN A TENT, HE'S REDUCED HIS OVERHEAD TO A HUNDREDTH OF MINE! HOW AM I SUPPOSED TO COMPETE WITH THAT?!
APOSTATES!
dust dust

YOU! THIS IS ALL YOUR FAULT!
M-M-ME?!
THE WHOLE LOT OF 'EM! APOSTATES!

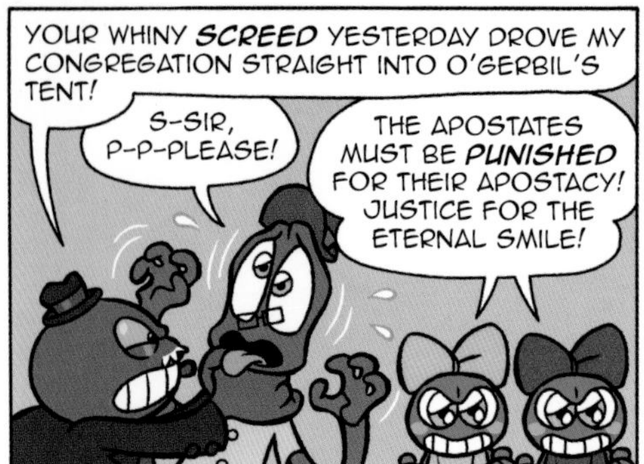
YOUR WHINY SCREED YESTERDAY DROVE MY CONGREGATION STRAIGHT INTO O'GERBIL'S TENT!
S-SIR, P-P-PLEASE!
THE APOSTATES MUST BE PUNISHED FOR THEIR APOSTACY! JUSTICE FOR THE ETERNAL SMILE!

IT'LL TAKE A MIRACLE TO GET THEM BACK NOW! IT'LL TAKE--
IT'S HIGH TIME FOR SOME--

--DIVINE RETRIBUTION!
THAT'S IT!

THAT'S WHAT WE'LL DO! WE'LL PUNISH THEM! WE'LL PUNISH THEM FOR BEING SO FICKLE!
COUGH! COUGH!
THE ETERNAL SMILE DESERVES IT! THE ETERNAL SMILE DEMANDS IT!

QUICK, FILBERT! DESIGN ME A CONTRAPTION LIKE THE WORLD HAS NEVER SEEN BEFORE! SOMETHING THAT'LL MAKE MY CONGREGATION COME RUNNING BACK TO ME WITH FISTFULS OF CASH!

SOMETHING THAT'LL BRING THE FURY OF HEAVEN DOWN ON SKINFLINT O'GERBIL'S MISERABLE LITTLE HEAD!

AFTER A FURIOUS MORNING OF BLUEPRINTS, JIGSAWS, AND HAMMERS, FILBERT FINALLY FULFILLS GRAN'PA GREENBAX'S OUTLANDISH REQUEST!
SHAKE A LEG, FILBERT, BEFORE O'GERBIL SQUEEZES EVERY LAST PENNY OUT OF THOSE DUPES!
C-C-COMING, SIR!
GLORY TO THE ETERNAL SMILE! GLORY TO THE ETERNAL SMILE FOREVER!

S-S-SIR, I D-D-DON'T TH-THINK YOU SHOULD W-W-WEAR THAT **ARMOR**. I DIDN'T D-D-DESIGN THE C-CATAPULT TO-
OH, STOP YOUR **BLUBBERING**, FILBERT!

THIS ARMOR GIVES ME JUST THE PIZZAZZ I NEED TO BECOME THE ETERNAL SMILE'S **ANGEL OF VENGEANCE!** ONE LOOK AT ME WILL SCARE THE QUARTERS RIGHT OUT OF THEIR POCKETS!
YES, YES! UNLEASH THE **FURY**, GRAN'PA!

NOW LIGHT MY SWORD ON FIRE!
W-W-WHAT? I'M N-NOT SO S-SURE-

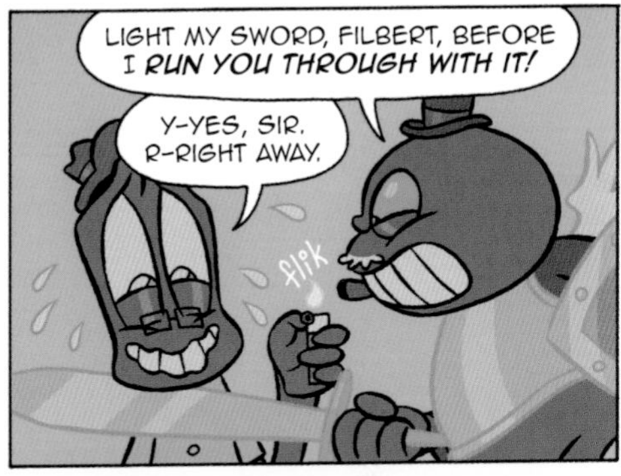
LIGHT MY SWORD, FILBERT, BEFORE I **RUN YOU THROUGH WITH IT!**
Y-YES, SIR. R-RIGHT AWAY.
flik

FWOOSH
THE ANGEL OF VENGEANCE IS READY!
SEMPITERNUS RISUS PETIMUS UT NOS VINDICES.

LAUNCH ON MY COUNT!
fwik

ONE!
TWO!
THREE!

VENGEANCE IS MINE!
SEMPITERNUS RISUS PETIMUS UT NOS VINDICES! SEMPITERNUS RISUS PETIMUS UT NOS VINDICES!

THUD!

FWOOSH
CROAK!

SIR!
GRAN'PA!
PUT IT OUT! PUT IT OUT!

FFSSCHHH

L-L-LUCKY I H-HAD T-THIS P-P-POCKET-SIZED F-FIRE EXTINGUISHER WITH M-ME!
COUGH! COUGH!

YOU IMBECILE!
N-NO, S-S-SIR, I DIDN'T M-MEAN T-- ACK!

I ASKED FOR *DIVINE RETRIBUTION!* A SPECTACLE THAT WOULD INSPIRE *AWE!* AND *THIS* IS WHAT YOU GIVE ME?!

I SHOULD'VE FIRED YOU LONG AGO, YOU NO-GOOD TALENTLESS HACK!

TO THINK I ACTUALLY PAID YOU A SALARY ALL THESE YEARS!

WHY, WHEN I'M THROUGH WITH YOU, YOU'LL WISH YOU WERE NEVER HATCHED!

CAN'T YOU GET ANYTHING RIGHT?!

YOU *EMBARRASSMENT!*

WHAT HAVE I DONE, FILBERT?! WHAT HAVE I DONE?!
HE'S DEAD. YOU'VE MURDERED HIM.

NO, NO! YOU GIRLS SAW IT, I WAS JUST HAVING A TALK WITH HIM, THAT'S ALL!
THE ETERNAL SMILE IS NOT PLEASED.
IT SHALL COME FOR YOU. JUSTICE WILL BE DONE.
THUMP

COME, POLLY, LET US CUT OUR TIES WITH THIS WRETCHED SOUL.
YES, MOLLY, LEST WE SHARE IN HIS DREADFUL FATE. GOODBYE, MR. GREENBAX.

MR. GREENBAX?! I'M YOUR GRAN'PA! GIRLS, PLEASE!
DON'T LEAVE ME, GIRLS! IT WASN'T SUPPOSED TO HAPPEN LIKE THIS! WE WERE JUST TALKING!
SEMPITERMUS RISUS PETIMUS UT NOS VINDICES.

WHAT AM I GOING TO DO?
WHAT AM I GOING TO DO?!

PLEASE, ETERNAL SMILE, YOU SAW WHAT HAPPENED! YOU KNOW MY HEART, DON'T YOU?!

IS IT SO WRONG FOR ME TO WANT THINGS DONE RIGHT?!

. . .

NO! NO! HAVE MERCY, PLEASE!

MERCY, PLEASE! *MERCY!*

CROAK!

CROAK!
CROAK!

CROAK!

CLICK!

Settle down, now, settle down.

It'll be all right, little guy.
We just can't have you killing the other characters. It's a children's show, after all.

Good thing we have everything on a five-minute time delay -- we were able to cut your little tirade out before it damaged our ratings.

Don't worry. This isn't going to hurt.
POP!

I'm sure this thing looks awfully frightening to you, but I just need to plug it into the chip on the top of your head.

Standard procedure for reprogramming your personality chip. We're going to take the aggression setting down a notch or two, okay?

What the--?!
PSSSSSS

Ack! You *pissed* on me, you little runt!

Oh no-- where'd you go? Where'd you go?!
Oh crap, he's gonna kill me gonna kill me gonna kill me--

How much longer 'til we're back on the air?
Boss wants to know.
Tell your uncle I'm working on it, okay?!

This doesn't look good, Norbert.
This doesn't look good at all. I think we need to notify Security.
No, no, please! I can handle this!

All security personnel: a character is loose in the building! I repeat, a character is loose in the building! Locate and detain immediately!

CLOP CLOP

HUFF HUFF
CLOP
CLOP
CLOP

?

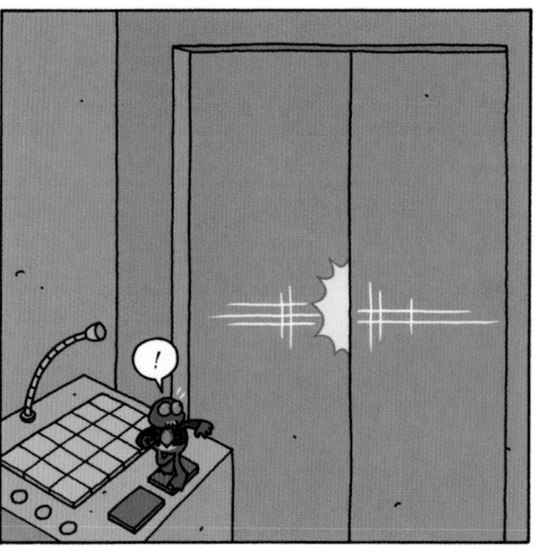
!

Should we check the theater there?
Not yet. Looks like there's a tour in progress.

HUFF
HUFF
HUFF

H-h-hello, b-boys and g-g-girls!
FILBERT...?

I'm F-Filbert Fr-Fr-Frog! You probably recognize me from *Frog Tales*, America's most popular childrens's show!

Welcome to the McFadden Studio Tour! Today you're going to see all the behind-the-scenes magic it takes to bring Frog Tales to your television screen!
McFadden
STUDIO TOUR

Over a decade ago, our founder Elias McFadden dreamgineered an ingenuous way of combining the unpredictable drama of reality TV with the anthropomorphic fun of Saturday morning cartoons: chip-enhanced animal characters!

By surgically attaching *McFadden Personality Chips* to the brains of real live animals, McFadden dreamgineers gave Gran'pa Greenbax, Molly, Polly, me, and all the other Frog Tales characters human-like speech, emotions, and personalities!

But that's not all! McFadden dreamgineers then built a giant synthetic environment in which we all live, work, and play, completely contained inside the McFadden Studio building!

That's right! Frogville, Bunnytown, and even the sites of Gran'pa Greenbax's most remote Profitable Adventures are all under the same roof you're under now!

Hidden cameras within the environment capture all the unpredictable action... and the unpredictable fun!

And my golly, what fun it's been! What started as a half hour after-school show has grown into a full-fledged 24-hour cable network!

And that's what makes *Frog Tales*, America's most popular children's show!

FROG TALES

Now if you'll follow your host through those doors to your right, you'll get your very first up-close glimpse of the city of Frogville!
Remember, no flash photography please!
S-s-see ya l-later, b-boys and g-g-girls!

Impressive, isn't it?

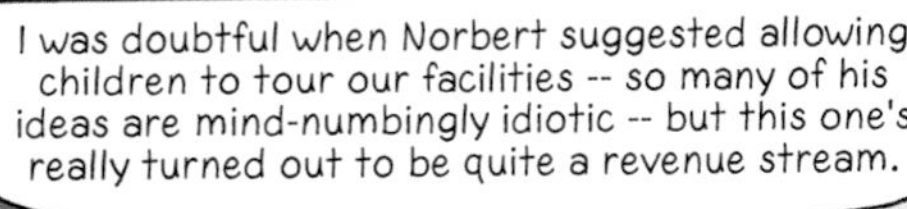
I was doubtful when Norbert suggested allowing children to tour our facilities -- so many of his ideas are mind-numbingly idiotic -- but this one's really turned out to be quite a revenue stream.

WH-WHO-- WHO--

No need to be afraid, Mr. Greenbax. Don't you recognize the cloth from which you're cut?
That chip so delicately embedded into your brain contains an algorithmic approximation of my personality -- a personality that has made *you* America's #1 children's entertainment property!

Elias McFadden. How do you do?

...and this is my office.
YOU'VE GOT QUITE AN OPERATION HERE, MR. McFADDEN! COLOR ME IMPRESSED!

Ha ha. Yes, well... There's a reason I brought you up here, Mr. Greenbax. I've a business proposal to make. Our show's been off the air now for forty-five minutes. It's the longest we've been off the air since we became a 24-hour cable channel three years ago. The phones have been ringing off the hook.

I need you back in Frogville, Mr. Greenbax. But I can't have you snap like that again, you understand? Death isn't very good for ratings in our target demographic.
I'M UNDER A LOT OF PRESSURE, MR. McFADDEN.

Yes, of course you are. Norbert wants to rewire you. Idiot. I say, why tamper with the perfect personality? Heh heh.

I know you, Mr. Greenbax. I know you as well as I know... well, ***me***. I know what makes you tick. I know you've been frustrated.
PUTTING UP WITH THOSE NUMBSKULLS DAY IN AND DAY OUT! AND THAT WEASEL ***O'GERBIL!*** CROAK! WITH CHARACTERS LIKE THAT RUNNNING AROUND, I DON'T KNOW WHAT I CAN PROMISE, MR. McFADDEN!

What if we made things easier on you, Mr. Greenbax? You think you could go back to Frogville and keep things... peaceful? What if we finally give you everything you've always wanted?
EVERYTHING?
Everything.

A ***FULL*** POOL O' CASH!
Done.

A POOL O' CASH ***BRIMMING OVER*** WITH MONEY!
Done.

A POOL O' CASH BRIMMING OVER WITH ***O'GERBIL'S*** MONEY!
Done, done, and ***done***.

It's out of the tradition of the show, but I'll have the dreamgineers rig a few of the sets in your favor. Just play your cards right and you'll have O'Gerbil's entire fortune by the end of the week.

Agreed?
WHY, THIS IS THE EASIEST DEAL I'VE EVER MADE! I LIKE THE WAY YOU THINK, MR. MCFADDEN!

Ha ha. Of course, you do. Now, Mr. Greenbax, if we can get back to--

THAT'S BEAUTIFUL. WHAT IS THAT?!
McFadden Pond. It used to be named after... some Indian or other. It was here when we first purchased the property. In fact, it's where we found you and the rest of the original cast. How about we--
THE SUNSET REFLECTING OFF THE SURFACE OF THE LAKE...

...MAKES IT LOOK GOLDEN.

Why, yes, I suppose it does. Come on, now, we want to get a jump on our next Profitable Adventure, don't we?

HOW DEEP DO YOU THINK IT IS?
What, the pond? I don't know! Mr. Greenbax, please--

DEEP ENOUGH FOR ME TO DIVE INTO AND NOT HIT MY HEAD ON THE BOTTOM?
How am I supposed to know?! Look, we've been off the air for almost an hour. I have sponsors, and we have a deal!

Do you hear me, Greenbax?! If you don't get back on that set this instant, I'm going to make O'Gerbil the star of the show!

Don't think I won't do it!
IT'S STRANGE...

... I NEVER IMAGINED IT WOULD FEEL SO GOOD TO REALIZE I'VE BEEN WRONG ALL ALONG.

I'm warning you, Greenbax!

Huh?! What do you think you're--!

CRASH!

Greenbax!

BOING!

SPLASH!

ZZZZT!

URGENT
REQUEST

COMMTECH

What are you milling around here for?

Oh! I-- well-- we had a meeting scheduled, sir, for one o'clock. My performance review.

Must've slipped my mind. I've been busy.

It's all right, really--

I'm not apologizing. I'm telling you:

I've been busy.

So. You've been here, what, five years--

Seven, sir.

--seven years. I've never had any complaints about your work. And I don't have any now.

Good job. You're a highly valued member of the CommTech team. Thanks for coming in.
Thank you, sir.

You're still here.

Well... there is another... um... I-- I saw the post for that open position on our website.

I just... I think I'm ready for new responsibilities. I've actually been taking some networking classes at night. I'm not... I mean, I really enjoy working here. It's been wonderful. I... I just...

Janet Oh, are you asking for a promotion?

Well...
...Yes, Mr. Hoffman. I suppose I am.

...
You see that plaque right there? I won it nine years ago by being the best phone sales associate in the company. The ***best.*** And this was when they started off-shoring to India, too. You know how many qualified phone sales associates they got over there? You have any idea how big that country is?
Uh... yes, sir. India's quite--

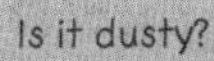
Is it dusty?
...India, sir?
No. The plaque. Is it dusty?
It might just be the lighting, but there seems to be a thin layer of--

SCRITCH
SCRATCH

You mind dusting it for me, Janet?
What? I... No. Not at all, sir.

RUB
RUB

HOO

Let me give it to you straight, Janet. Money's tight. True, we've had a good quarter. A great quarter, in fact -- a great quarter under great leadership. But if we want those great quarters to keep coming, we have to watch that bottom line, you understand?
But I like you. I mean, we were just saying, you've been a loyal employee of this company for the last five years--
--seven--

--seven years. I'll make it my personal mission to see what I can do. How's that sound to you?
Thank you, Mr. Hoffman.

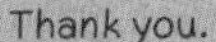
Thank you.

click

From: Reginald Hoffman
Subject: YOUR PROMOTION

!

From: Reginald Hoffman
Subject: YOUR PROMOTION

Dear Janet,

After giving your request considerable thought, I have some bad news: I'm going to have to say "no" to your promotion. :-(

Even so, you are a highly valued member of the CommTech team!

Mr. Hoffman
Regional Director
Phone Sales Associate of the Year 1998
CommTech Internet Services, Inc.

P.S. There is a box of donuts in the break room. Help yourself! :-)

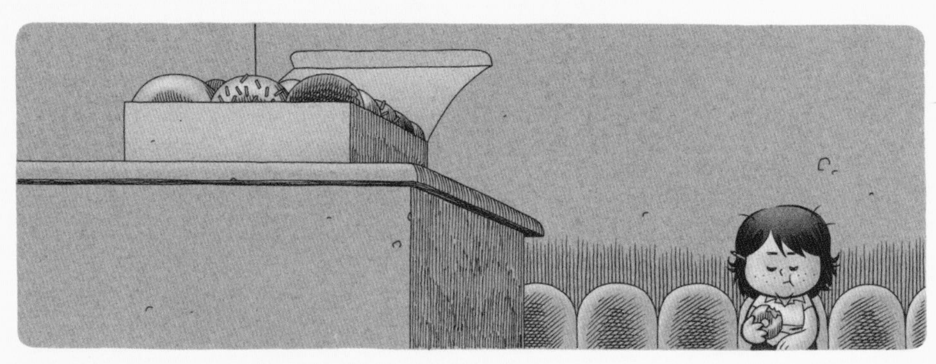

Janet Oh,

I change your lock to fix door sticking problem.

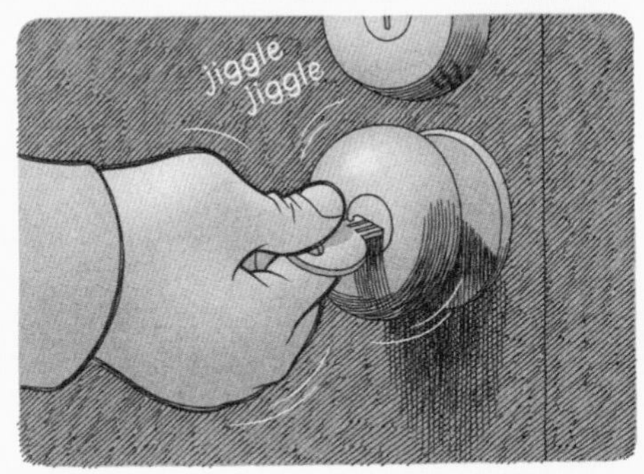

I bring you new key tonight.
Be here waiting for me.
Stan
sigh

...please leave a message at the beep.

Thank you.
PIZZA

203

COMMTECH

Dear Friend,

I heartily solicit for your honest/Godly assistance to save my family's soul. Since the death of my father the late former Nigeria head of state, I no longer trust anybody within my beloved country.

You have heard from media reports of various huge sums of money deposited by my father in security firms abroad. US $350,000,000 of this must be immediately transferred to United States for safekeeping.

Might you have a bank account of use? I require simply your routing number and PIN. For your trouble, you will please accept my humble gift of 10% of total sum for yours to keep.

I got your contacts through my personal research and found trust in you. Out of desperation, my family decided to reach you. Please help.

Sincerely yours,

Prince Henry Alembu
Royal Family of Nigeria

I'm flattered, Prince Alembu, but I don't know... I mean, we haven't even met--
Please, Janet. I am in need of you.

"I saw th-th-the open p-position on our w-w-website and--
poof!

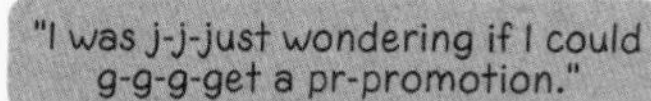
"I was j-j-just wondering if I could g-g-g-get a pr-promotion."

Ha ha!
#1 BOSS

That was the longest sentence I ever heard her say. I thought she was gonna wet herself.

So did you give it to her?

No, course not. I don't wanna be mean or anything, but she's just so... so... what's the word--

Awkward? Shy? Frumpy?

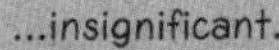

Dear Prince Henry Alembu,

It would be an honor to help you and your family. You will find my bank account information in the attached document. Thank you for entrusting me with a task of such significance.

Your friend,
Janet Oh

Send

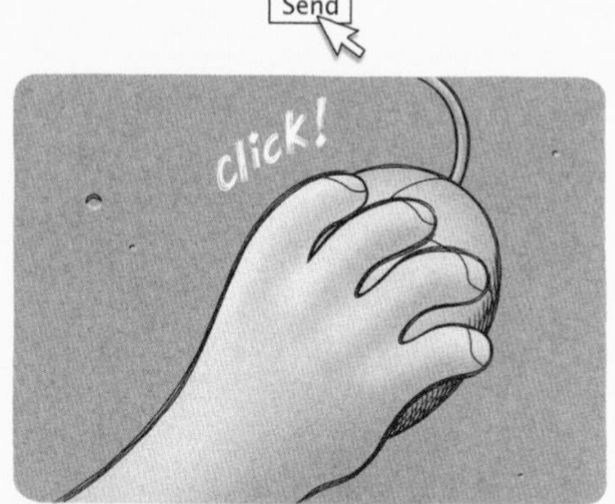

Prince Alembu,

I visited an ATM machine on my lunch break. Imagine my surprise to find my checking account completely cleaned out.

I suppose I shouldn't be angry. After all, I have been betrayed by nothing more than my own naive generosity.

Janet

COMMTECH

Ding! You have mail.
?

From: Henry Alembu
Subject: RE: URG T REQUEST
click
click

Dear Janet,

Do not misunderstand my intentions please. Politics here are excessive instability and my family suddenly was in need of emergency funds.

To use your personal monies was a last resort. US $350,000,000 to be forthcoming. For now, might you lend another $500?

Sincerely yours,
Prince Henry Alembu

Reply

Prince Henry Alembu,

I underestimated your family's plight.
All is forgiven.

Janet,

I have no words to express my appreciation of our friendship. You have saved us much hardship/torture.

All of royal family in Nigeria lies prostrate in debt to you.

Might you be willing to expand our debt by $500 more? Medicinal supplies for my elderly aunt.

Sincerely yours,
Prince Henry Alembu

Dear Prince Henry,

It is good to hear from you again. You will have the money by tomorrow.

Please give your aunt my warmest regards and thank her for her patience.

How far away is that from Nigeria?

Tell me, Prince Henry, what is Nigeria like?

Love,
Janet

Dear Janet,

In this season the Nigerian night skies are utmost in clarity. The brightness of the stars reminds me of your superb humanity.

Only by your help have my family and I been able to thrive. Soon, I will be transferring the $350,000,000.

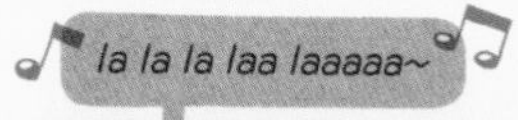
la la la laa laaaaa~

Please, one more favor. Another $1000?

Sincerely yours,
Henry

Dear Henry,

I blush at the sweetness of your words.

If you can wait until my next paycheck at the end of the month, I shall fulfill your request.

In the meantime, please give your family my best. You are always in my thoughts.

Love,
Janet

Dearest Janet,

My heart bursts from your generosity. I bear most excellent news!

By grace/fortune, my visa and papers have come through. I have now the chance to visit to your country, to finalize US $350,000,000 transfer in person.

Only $2,500 for airfare is required.

Your prince always,
Henry

My sweet prince,
That truly is most excellent news. Before granting you this final favor, however, I must ask for one in return.
tk
tk
tk tk

Will you promise to meet me in person as soon as you arrive in the United States?
Love always,
Janet
tk
tk
tk tk

Working late, Janet?
Yes.

Ding! You have mail.

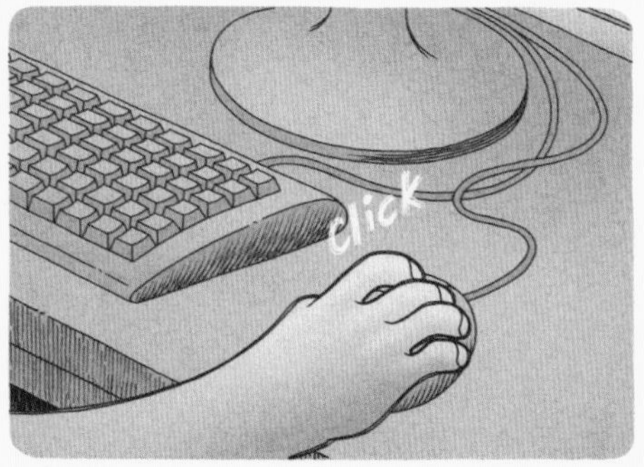
click

My dearest friend of my heart,

Name the place and time. I will be there.
I tremble with anticipation/joy.

Yours as always,
Henry

Dearest Henry,

There is an Ethiopian restaurant just down the street from where I work...

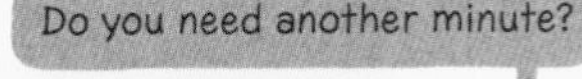

Blue Nile

I'm sorry, Miss, but our
kitchen closes in 10 minutes.
Is there anything I can get you?

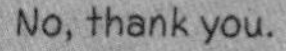
No, thank you.

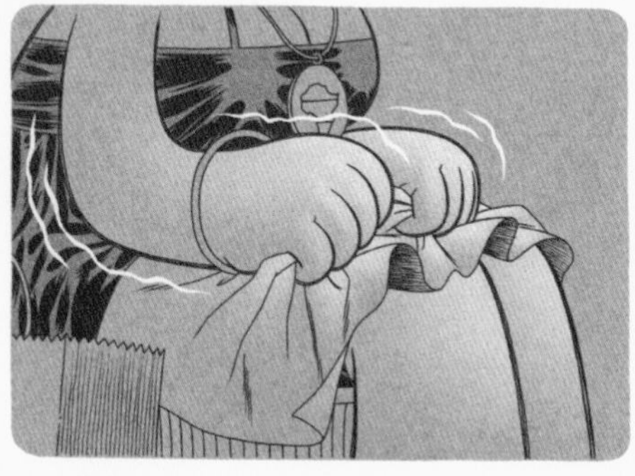

Blue Nile ETHIOPI RESTAURA
TAXI

TAXI
WELCOME
TO
PACIFICA
STATE
UNIVERSITY

BOWLES
MEN'S
DORMITORY

167
KNOCK!
KNOCK!

Crap, man! I'm in the middle of WoW, for cryin' out--
Well, *hello.* What can I do for you?
167
NO FAT CHICKS

I'd like to speak with Prince Henry Alembu.

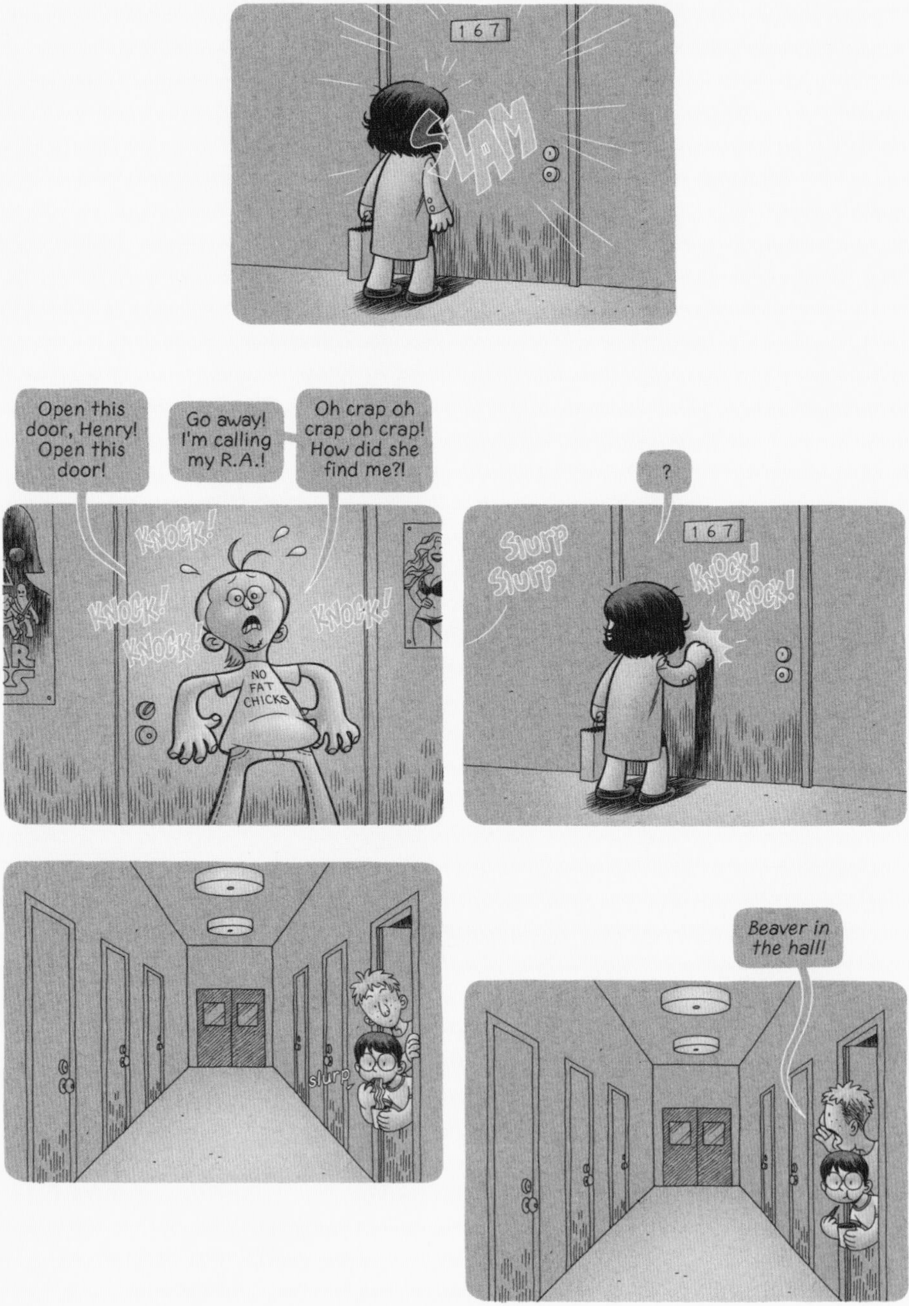

Open this door, Henry! Open this door!

Go away! I'm calling my R.A.!

Oh crap oh crap oh crap! How did she find me?!

KNOCK! KNOCK! KNOCK! KNOCK!

NO FAT CHICKS

?

167

Slurp Slurp

KNOCK! KNOCK!

slurp

Beaver in the hall!

slurp

167

Open this door, Henry! After all the money I've given, I deserve a date with a Nigerian prince!
167
BAM! BAM!

A date?

Do it, Steve!
But she's a nut job!
Dude! She's a girl, and he's *Steve!*

All right. Where are we going?

You go, boy-eee!
Someone's gettin' some tonight!
Boom chicka waa waa!

Put this on.

Denny's
Denny's

Come on!
This isn't--
Look, you want to do this or not?

Two, please.

mnch mnch

This is a dinner date. *Eat.*

Man, this is boss! I forgot how tasty Denny's Grand Slam breakfast is! I don't think I've had one of these since I took my cousin to the prom!
slurp
crunch
slurp

Oh, uh... When I say "cousin" I mean in the general sense, you know? Not... uh... you know? Heh heh.
...

So, Henry--
My name's not Henry, actually. It's Steve.
So, *Henry*, tell me about Nigeria.

Ooo-kay...

Well... it's, um, really sunny there. With big... you know, trees. And animals. Lots of animals.
Animals? That sounds wonderful. I love animals. What sort of species?

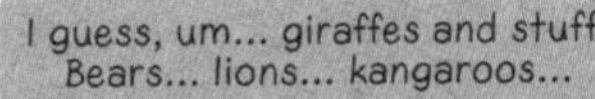

≶sigh≶ I can't do this. Look, I'm sorry... about everything. Sometimes, when you do stuff on the Internet, when you don't see the other person...

I'll pay for dinner, okay? Order dessert for yourself, too. My cousin loves-- er, I heard they got a great key lime pie. Is that cool?
But, Prince Henry--!

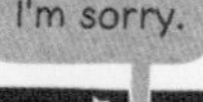
I'm sorry.

Henry! You're not even done with your dinner yet!

But-- but--

≷sigh≶
W-wait.
Wait!
Why... I mean...
what'd you do with
all that m-money?

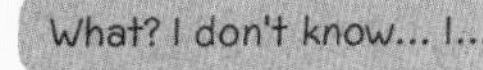
What? I don't know... I...

Steve, please. No
more lies. Just tell me.

. . .

Start-up
capital.
ZIIIP!

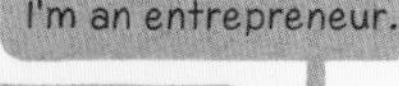
I'm an entrepreneur.

What kind of business?

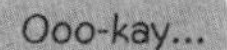

You ever heard of Second Life? It's like this whole *virtual reality* you can get to from the Internet. You walk around in this cartoon character called an *avatar*, and you can do anything. Well, *almost* anything. See, avatars don't have... private parts. Heh heh.
Ooo-kay...

So that's what my company does. We create "avatar enhancements" for "adult leisure activities" in digital environments.

You used my money to make genitals for a video game?

No no no! Second Life is *not* a video game! That is *such* a misconception! It's like this other *dimension*, okay?! It's so much more than--

≈sigh≈ Forget it.

How'd you find me, anyway?
I work for CommTech. We manage your school's net-work and Internet services.

I don't get it, then. You must've known, right? This whole time--

Look, Ma! I'm a boy wizard!

Steve, you idiot! Give me back my bathrobe!

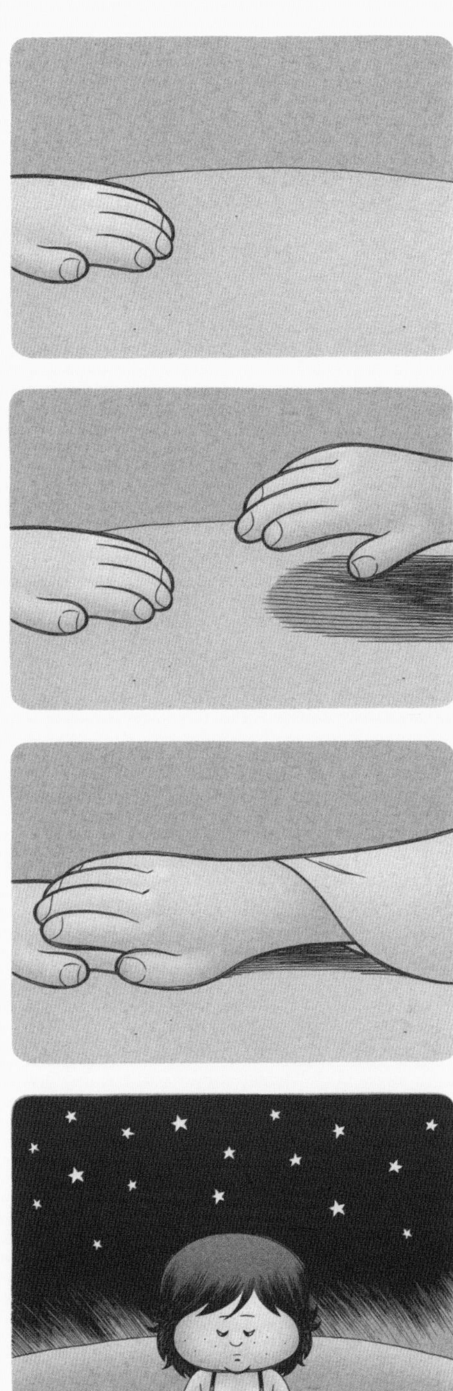

Yes. I know.

Come with me.

My fellow countrymen, I present to you my beloved bride--

--and the new
Queen of Nigeria!

!

KNOCK!
KNOCK!

Dear queen, what's the matter?
KNOCK! KNOCK!

I'm no queen. They all know it. I must look ridiculous in these clothes.

Don't be foolish, my love! My family has been restored to power! I am now king, and you are my bride! You are rightfully the queen!

Henry, listen to me. I'm not a queen. I'm an office assistant.

Stop. Stop!
I don't live in a castle. I work in a cubicle
COMMTECH

You, this place, our life together... it's all so beautiful... but it isn't real. I don't even think Nigeria has a royal family. All of this is just a... an escape.

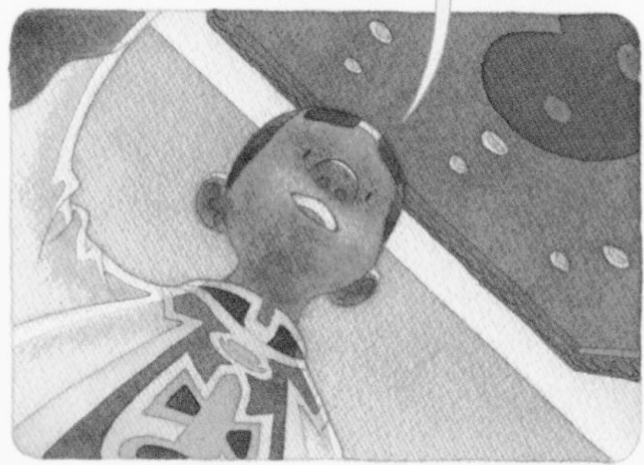
You... you are right about many things. But you are wrong about why you are here. You did not come here to *escape*, but to *see*.

Some truths can only be seen clearly beneath the light of the Nigerian sun.

Open the door. Come out. I will show you.

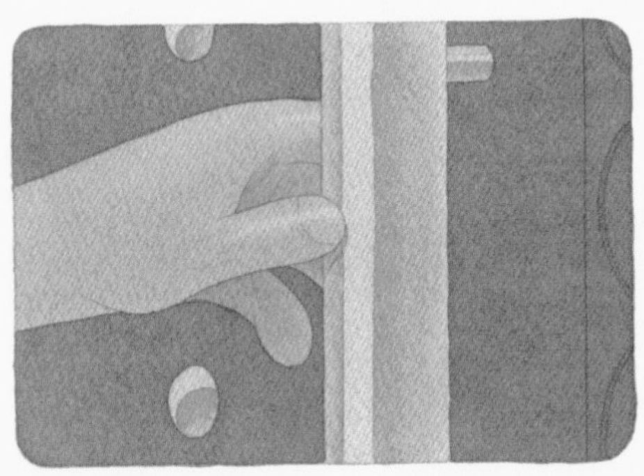

Once again, my fellow countrymen,
I present to you my beloved bride--

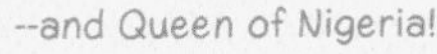
--and Queen of Nigeria!

...Hi.

CLAP
CLAP
CLAP
CLAP
CLAP

YEAH!
CLAP
WHOO-HOO!
CLAP
CLAP
CLAP
CLAP
WOO!
YAY!
CLAP
CLAP

CLAP
CLAP
CLAP

CLAP
CLAP
CLAP
YEAH!
CLAP
YEAH!
CLAP
WOO-HOO!

ALL HAIL THE QUEEN!

Sorry.
No, no. It's okay.

You want a bite of my scramble?
No thanks.
Can I have a sip of your Sprite, then?

OWLES
MEN'S
RMITORY

So, uh... You want to come up?
No thanks.

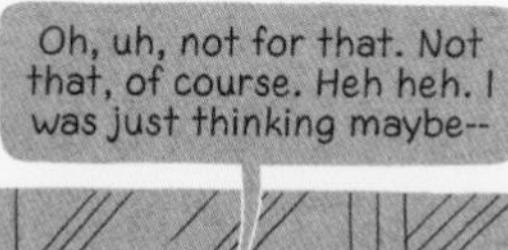
Oh, uh, not for that. Not that, of course. Heh heh. I was just thinking maybe--

No thanks.

It's just that I've got this pretty boss collection of vintage Micronauts action figures. Maybe you'd--
No thanks.

All right. Heh heh.

You know, all that money-- I really see it as more of a loan. Once NeoNads, Inc., starts turning a profit, I'm gonna pay it all back, okay?

It shouldn't be too long. Just last week I got this order for a fourteen inch--
Thanks for coming out with me, Steve. I enjoyed it.

Oh, yeah. Yeah. Me too.

So maybe next time on the Micronauts?
I'll see you around. Thanks again.

12345

12345
Ding!

My dearest Henry,

I miss you, my king. I think back often to our days together in Nigeria. It never fails to make me smile.

Life looks so different now. It's as if you've given me a piece of myself that I've always longed for, but never quite knew how to find.

You are forever in my heart, Henry.
Thank you for everything.

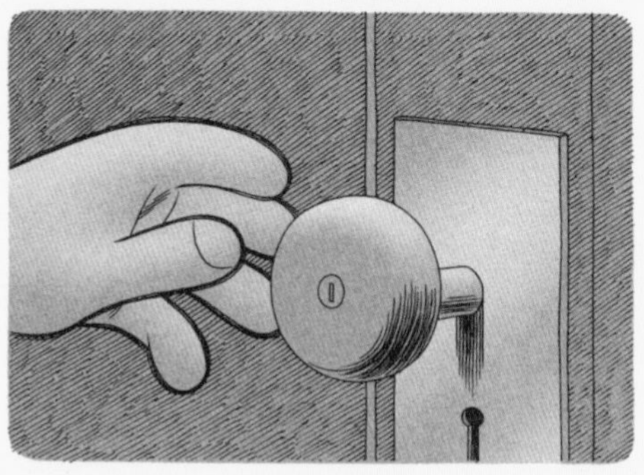

Your queen,

Janet Oh

Mr. Hoffman,
we need to talk.

Michael L. Printz Award
National Book Award Finalist

Eisner Award for Best Graphic Album
Reuben Award for Best Graphic Novel
Amazon.com Best Graphic Novel of the Year
American Library Association Top Ten Book for Young Adults
YALSA Top Ten Graphic Novel for Teens
Booklist Editor's Choice Book
Booklist Top Ten Graphic Novel for Youth
Publisher's Weekly Best Book of the Year
Publisher's Weekly Comics Week Best Comic of the Year
School Library Journal Best Book of the Year
NPR Holiday Pick
Bank Street Best Children's Book of the Year
NYPL Book for the Teen Age
San Francisco Chronicle Best Book of the Year
Library Media Editor's Choice for 2007
Chinese American Librarians Association Best Book Award

"Like Toni Morrison's *The Bluest Eye* and Laurence Yep's *Dragonwings*, this novel explores the impact of the American dream on those outside the dominant culture in a finely wrought story that is an effective combination of humor and drama."
– *School Library Journal*, starred review

"Yang accomplishes the remarkable feat of practicing what he preaches with this book: accept who you are and you'll already have reached out to others."
– *Publisher's Weekly*

"The stories have a simple, engaging sweep to them, but their weighty subjects—shame, racism, and friendship—receive thoughtful, powerful examination."
– *Booklist*

"This graphic novel could be especially cathartic for teens and adults of Asian descent, but people of any ethnicity would find themselves reflected in the universal themes of self-acceptance, peer pressure, and racial tensions."
– *VOYA*

A.L.I.E.E.E.N.
BY LEWIS TRONDHEIM

THE LOST COLONY
VOL. 1
BY GRADY KLEIN

THE LOST COLONY
VOL. 2
BY GRADY KLEIN

THE LOST COLONY
VOL. 3
BY GRADY KLEIN

TOWN BOY
BY LAT

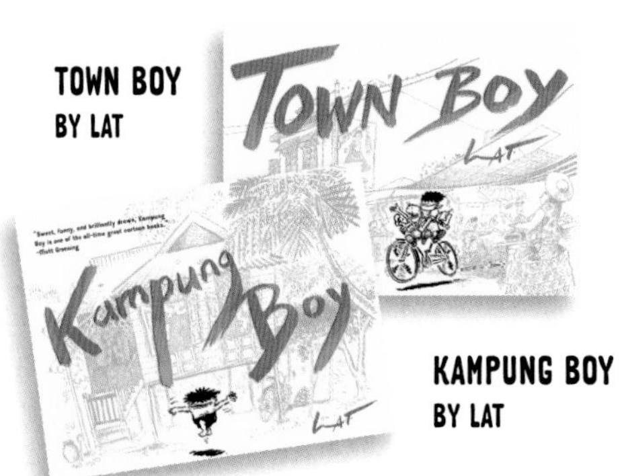

KAMPUNG BOY
BY LAT

THE PROFESSOR'S DAUGHTER
BY EMMANUEL GUIBERT & JOANN SFAR

ROBOT DREAMS
BY SARA VARON

KLEZMER
BY JOANN SFAR

THE BLACK DIAMOND DETECTIVE AGENCY
BY EDDIE CAMPBELL

LAIKA
BY NICK ABADZIS

VAMPIRE LOVES
BY JOANN SFAR

The First Second Collection

THREE SHADOWS
BY CYRIL PEDROSA

LIFE SUCKS
BY JESSICA ABEL, GABE SORIA, & WARREN PLEECE

ALAN'S WAR
BY EMMANUEL GUIBERT

BOURBON ISLAND
BY APPOLLO & LEWIS TRONDHEIM

GUS
BY CHRIS BLAIN

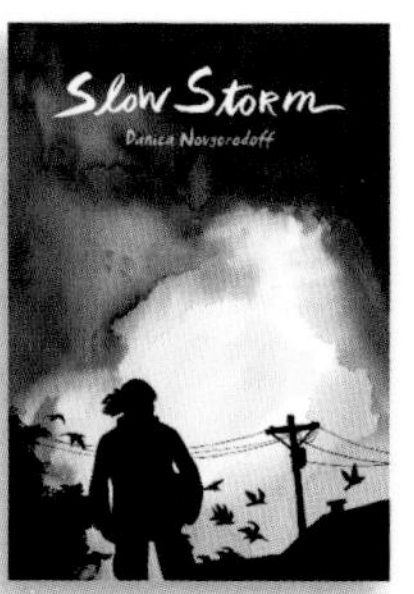

SLOW STORM
BY DANICA NOVGORODOFF

PRINCE OF PERSIA
BY JORDAN MECHNER, A.B. SINA, LEUYEN PHAM, & ALEX PUVILLAND

THE AMAZING REMARKABLE MONSIEUR LEOTARD
BY EDDIE CAMPBELL & DAN BEST

GARAGE BAND
BY GIPI

NOTES FOR A WAR STORY
BY GIPI

New York & London

Published by First Second
First Second is an imprint of Roaring Brook Press,
a division of Holtzbrinck Publishing Holdings Limited Partnership
175 Fifth Avenue, New York, NY 10010

Distributed in Canada by H. B. Fenn and Company Ltd.
Distributed in the United Kingdom by Macmillan Children's Books,
a division of Pan Macmillan.

Duncan's Kingdom was previously published by Image Comics in 1999.

Design by Danica Novgorodoff

Color Assistance on *Duncan's Kingdom* and *Gran'pa Greenbax and the Eternal Smile* by Elena Diaz

Cataloging-in-Publication Data is on file at the Library of Congress.

ISBN-13: 978-1-59643-156-0
ISBN-10: 1-59643-156-3

First Second books are available for special promotions and premiums.
For details, contact: Director of Special Markets, Holtzbrinck Publishers.

First Edition May 2009
Printed in China
1 3 5 7 9 10 8 6 4 2